THE SECRET
TREASURE

THE SECRET TREASURE

LEAGUE OF GRIEFERS
BOOK ONE

Winter Morgan

Sky Pony Press
New York

Copyright © 2015 by Hollan Publishing, Inc.

Sky Pony Press books may be purchased in bulk at special discounts for sales promotion, corporate gifts, fund-raising, or educational purposes. Special editions can also be created to specifications. For details, contact the Special Sales Department, Sky Pony Press, 307 West 36th Street, 11th Floor, New York, NY 10018 or info@skyhorsepublishing.com.

Sky Pony® is a registered trademark of Skyhorse Publishing, Inc.®, a Delaware corporation.

Minecraft® is a registered trademark of Notch Development AB. The Minecraft game is copyright © Mojang AB.

Visit our website at www.skyponypress.com.

10 9 8 7 6 5 4 3 2

Library of Congress Cataloging-in-Publication Data is available on file.

Cover photo by Megan Miller

Print ISBN: 978-1-63450-593-2
Ebook ISBN: 978-1-63450-594-9

Printed in Canada

TABLE OF CONTENTS

THE SECRET TREASURE

1
PROTECTORS OF THE OVERWORLD

Violet rushed through the dense forest, tripping over the roots of a tree. "Ouch," she said, rubbing her leg.

"Are you okay?" Noah stopped.

"I think so," she said. But Violet was in pain.

"We have to keep going. They're coming after us. We don't have much time." Noah was worried.

Violet pulled a potion of swiftness from her inventory and took a gulp. "I think I can make it. But what's our plan?"

Noah looked behind them; a gang of five rainbow men carrying diamond swords was approaching. "Our plan? Run!"

Violet handed Noah some of her potion. He drank and the two sprinted through the forest, trying to escape from their enemy.

"I don't see them," Violet looked back. "Do you?"

Noah took a quick glance. "No, I don't either. But I don't trust them. We have to keep moving."

Noah and Violet had been exploring the fields and caves outside their village when the pesky rainbow griefers arrived. Every day their village lived in fear of Daniel and his league of powerful griefers. Noah and Violet were tired of the attacks. Recently, the attacks were becoming more severe, and this one was particularly harsh. Usually when Daniel and his band of bullies approached them, they would hand over whatever treasure they found or resources they had, and the griefers would take it and leave. This time Violet had offered the griefers potatoes and an emerald, but they shot an arrow at her anyway. When Noah came to her aid, one of the rainbow griefers struck him with a diamond sword and demanded everything in his inventory.

Reluctantly handing over diamonds, a sword, and armor, Noah said, "Please, leave us alone."

The griefer laughed and struck him again.

Violet and Noah sprinted away, but the determined griefers had trailed behind them. Now the pair looked back and realized the griefers were no longer following them. They were finally far enough from the village that they felt safe. They had reached a sandy beach; it was the perfect spot for a restful holiday vacation, but this wasn't a time to rejoice. Noah and Violet were exhausted and upset.

Violet said, "Noah, I don't want to run anymore."

"What else can we do?" asked Noah.

"I want to fight," replied Violet. "I know we can out-wit Daniel. He might have a lot of griefers working with him, but we're smart. We need to come up with a plan to save our village from Daniel."

Noah looked out at the water and walked along the sandy beach. He thought about Violet's proposal. "But they stole my armor and my diamonds. I don't have very much left."

"I've been hiding a lot of resources," Violet told her friend. "I think we can do it."

"Do what? You mean actually stage an attack on Daniel? We aren't that powerful."

"But we have to try. Nobody else is fighting back and our village is being destroyed. I can't watch this anymore. I want to live in a peaceful village," pleaded Violet.

"Maybe we should move?" suggested Noah.

"And abandon everyone we know? Let them deal with the wrath of Daniel and the griefers? I couldn't live with that guilt. I couldn't build a new home, know-ing all the people I cared about were being threatened every day."

The sun was beginning to set. Noah and Violet were far from home.

"We need to find shelter," said Noah, looking at the setting sun. He knew that in minutes mobs would be crawling around this serene beach, targeting him and Violet.

"Don't worry. I can build something," Violet reas-sured Noah.

"Great—you're the best person for the job." Noah was excited to help his friend. Despite the awful circumstances, he was happy to see Violet building again.

Violet was a master builder. Before the rainbow griefers took over, she had been invited to partake in building competitions all around the Overworld. But once the rainbow griefers invaded their peaceful town, the townspeople weren't allowed to leave. Before the invasion, people would travel from all around the Overworld to see Violet's home. She lived in a tree house that she had designed herself. Besides being skillfully designed, it also had a fantastic view. Their village was located in the Jungle Biome, and her house was high atop a tree overlooking the water.

She had also built a tree house for Noah, who was her best friend. She had even built a small footbridge that connected their homes. The twin tree houses attracted a lot of attention. People would ask her all about how she had built them, and would request tours. However, once the griefers settled in their village, the questions stopped coming, and so did the building competitions. People stayed away from their village. It wasn't a safe place. The entire Overworld knew about Daniel and his griefers. And now that her town was filled with violence, Violet had no time to build. Her life wasn't about intricately designed homes; it was about survival.

Now Violet brushed up on her rusty building skills to construct a crude cabin. It took very little time to make, offering just the bare necessities to survive the night—shelter and a bed. By the time night had set in, they were safely tucked away underneath their red wool blankets. Before heading to bed, Noah lit a torch and left it on the door so hostile mobs wouldn't come near their small makeshift home.

When morning finally arrived, Violet got out of bed. Noah was already up. He was preparing some breakfast.

"I found these apples the other day. I can't believe I was able to hide them from Daniel." Noah offered one to Violet.

"Thanks," she said, taking a bite. "I just want you to know, when I was talking about fighting the griefers, I was serious."

"You mentioned that you have supplies. What do you have?"

Violet rattled off a long list of supplies, from potions to diamonds. "See? We can do it. We just have to come up with a plan."

"But how did you hide all of those supplies?" Noah was shocked.

With a sly smile, Violet replied, "I have my ways."

"How?" Noah insisted.

"I hide everything in a chest in my house."

"But that's not safe. They are always breaking into people's homes."

Violet said quite confidently, "Don't worry. It's all booby trapped."

"Wow! No way!" Noah exclaimed, impressed with her clever thinking.

"Once we get back home, I'll share everything with you. We can outfit ourselves with great armor and weapons, and plan our attack. We will become warriors."

"I'm not sure I'm cut out to be a warrior." As Noah said these words, the four rainbow griefers that had been following them ripped the hinge from the cabin door and showered Noah and Violet with arrows.

Narrowly avoiding being hit, Violet was able to build a wall with a few blocks and then grabbed Noah. "Quick, hide behind here."

"We know where you're hiding." The griefer laughed. "It's just a matter of time before we destroy you."

Violet handed Noah armor and a sword. "Sometimes you don't have a choice what you become. Sometimes you just have to do it."

2
BURIED BOOKS

"I can't go out there," stuttered Noah. "I'm not a fighter."

"Don't worry—I've got this." Violet grabbed a block of TNT and threw it over the wall at the griefers.

Kaboom! Parts of the wall fell on Violet and Noah. They brushed away the rubble and looked out at the small empty room.

"We destroyed them!" exclaimed Noah.

"See? You are a warrior," Violet told him.

"But you're the one who threw the TNT."

"It doesn't matter. We're in this together." Violet walked out the front door and Noah followed.

"Not so fast!" a voice called out.

A large rainbow griefer approached Violet and Noah, holding out his diamond sword.

"Don't point that at me," threatened Violet.

"You have destroyed my friends. And you have upset Daniel. He doesn't like to lose any soldiers." The rainbow griefer stood in front of Violet.

"Soldiers!" Violet laughed. "Is that what he calls them? Because I call them bullies and criminals."

"Now that you've defeated a few of our men, you think you're very strong. Don't be overly confident. This is one battle you'll never win." The rainbow griefer struck Violet with his sword.

Noah lunged at the rainbow griefer. With every ounce of energy in his body, he hit him with his diamond sword. Then he pulled out a potion bottle and splashed a potion of harming on the griefer. The griefer became weak and couldn't fight back. Noah delivered a final blow, and defeated the evil griefer.

"Noah, that's fantastic." Violet was thrilled. Noah was learning to defend himself.

"I couldn't see him hurt you," Noah told his friend.

"See? You are a warrior." Violet smiled.

"I guess so." Noah shrugged.

"We have to head back to the village. If Daniel knows we've destroyed five of his men, he is going to retaliate. I don't want him blowing up our tree houses. If he does that, we'll lose all of the valuable resources I've hidden in the chest," said Violet.

Noah and Violet walked back to the village. Just when the iron golem that sat by the village shops was in sight, Noah stumbled upon an opening to a cave.

"Wow, I've never seen this cave before," said Noah.

"I don't think we have time to explore. We have to head back to the village—I'm worried about our homes. I don't trust Daniel."

"But maybe we can find something in here that will help us defeat Daniel," suggested Noah.

Violet knew that he was right; there could be diamonds or emeralds they could mine, and they needed supplies, badly.

They lit torches and entered the cave. It was dark, and a cave spider crept between their feet. Noah hit the spider with his diamond sword.

"I don't see anything here." Violet dug her pickaxe into the ground, but it was barren. There was nothing to mine.

"Yes, it looks like this cave has already been looted," Noah agreed.

The two friends were walking toward the exit when they saw a chest hidden in the dark corner.

"Noah, do you see that chest?" Violet thought she was imagining it.

"Yes . . . what is it?" Noah held his breath as he slowly opened the chest. He was worried it could be a trap set by a griefer, and might explode when he opened it.

"Oh, wow!" Violet exclaimed. "Look at this." She pulled out a shiny brown book tied with red ribbon.

"It's an enchanted book." Noah leafed through the pages.

"This is going to come in very handy." Violet looked at the book. "It must be extremely powerful—look at all of the items we can enchant with it."

"But we don't have an anvil." Noah knew that would be vital to enchanting armor and weapons.

"I do!" Violet said happily. "It's hidden in my house."

"We need to get back to the tree houses." Noah grabbed the book and placed it in his inventory.

Walking toward the exit, Noah and Violet could hear voices. They hid in a dark corner, keeping a sharp eye out for cave spiders as they listened to the people who entered the cave.

"Oh no!" Noah said in a quiet whisper. "It's rainbow griefers." His heart began to pound and Violet hoped they couldn't hear it. She knew there was no way Noah could control his heart racing. He was nervous. She took a deep breath and stood by her friend, watching as the two rainbow griefers explored the dark cave.

"Where is it?" the rainbow griefer asked his companion. "Are you sure Daniel said the chest is in this cave?"

"Yes, we have to find the chest. If we come back empty handed, Daniel will be furious," replied the other rainbow griefer.

"What's in the chest that's so valuable?" questioned the first griefer.

"Daniel claims this chest has the most powerful enchanted book in the Overworld. The other rainbow griefers hid it here during an attack." The second griefer searched the cave some more.

Violet watched their feet walk by. She contemplated attacking the griefers, but they passed without noticing the two thieves hiding in the dark corner.

"I found it!" one of the griefers called out.

Violet could see them both hurry over to the chest.

"It's been opened!" The griefer was shocked. His colorful body shone in the dark cave.

"Somebody has stolen Daniel's book. They are going to pay."

"But who could have found it?" the first griefer questioned.

"I don't know, but Daniel will find out. He is extremely powerful. Nobody can hide from him."

Both griefers agreed that Daniel was powerful and whoever was in possession of the book would suffer.

Noah's heart beat faster. Then he dropped his sword.

"Who's there!" one of the griefers called out.

"I see them! I see the thieves," the other griefer shouted.

But the day was ending and a creeper lurked through the entrance of the cave. The griefers tried to sprint, but they couldn't get out of the way in time. The creeper exploded.

Kaboom!

"I hope they couldn't see our faces." Noah was terrified.

"I'm sure it will be okay," Violet reassured her friend, trying to believe the words as she said them.

3
COLORFUL CATASTROPHES

Violet and Noah sprinted toward the village and their tree houses. They worried the rainbow griefers they had defeated in the cabin might have respawned and begun searching for them. When they finally reached the tree houses, Noah and Violet climbed up the wooden ladders and watched for the rainbow griefers that might be trailing behind them.

"I think we're okay," Noah said as he looked out from the entrance. Noah and Violet had a panoramic view of the village and the water, so they could watch to see if the rainbow griefers were coming down any of the streets toward their home.

As Violet opened the door to her house, she was shot with an arrow.

Noah's heart began to thump. *I can do this. I can do this*, he told himself. Violet struck one of the griefers with her diamond sword.

"Get a potion, Noah. Help!" she called to her friend.

Noah grabbed a potion of weakness and crossed the footbridge to Violet's tree house. As soon as he was inside, he threw it on the two menaces in Violet's living room.

The rainbow griefers were weakened. Violet knew this was a small victory.

"Tell Daniel he won't win this war!" Violet screamed at the rainbow griefer as she hit him with her sword.

Noah, too, used his sword to hit the griefers until they were defeated.

"Wow, you're a really good fighter," said Violet, putting her sword away.

Noah was shocked. He had had no idea that he would be able to win that battle. "Thanks," he said rather humbly.

"We have to see if they stole our supplies and then get out of here fast. They know this is where we live. We can't stay here. We have to get the stuff and go." Violet hoped the chest was still in her bedroom. She remembered it was booby-trapped, so if the griefers even attempted to open the chest, they would have activated the pistons and fallen through the wooden floor to the ground below. She hadn't noticed any griefers on the ground, so she hoped it was okay.

"And we need to enchant our swords," added Noah.

"Yes—let me get the anvil." Violet sprinted to the corner where she kept the chest.

"Okay, where is it?" Noah was feeling anxious and wanted to be prepared for the next attack.

"It's here!" Violet was excited. She opened the chest and found all the valuables she had secured.

Before they could unearth the treasures, there was a loud explosion.

Kaboom!

The tree house shook.

"What was that?" Noah's voice quivered.

Violet rushed to the front door, peering across the footbridge that connected their houses.

"They blew up your house. And I'm pretty sure this one is going to be next." Violet was devastated. She had put so much into building the house and now it was gone. But she didn't have time to mourn the loss.

"I know this is awful, but we can't get upset. We have to gather all the resources from this chest and place them in our inventory before they blow up this house too." Violet quickly grabbed diamonds, an anvil, armor, potions, and all the other supplies she had stored in the chest with Noah's help. When they were done, they suited up in the best diamond armor.

"We can't lose this book," Noah reminded Violet, as he held the enchanted book tightly in his arms.

"I know. We have to find a place outside of town where we can enchant everything and prepare for battle," Violet said as they rushed out the door.

Violet was relieved that the ladder wasn't damaged. They crawled down the ladder, but once they reached the ground, an army of rainbow griefers met them.

"We're outnumbered. There's nothing we can do!" Noah was ready to surrender.

"Yes, there is." Violet splashed a potion of invisibility on them, and the two sprinted as fast as they could out of the town.

The rainbow griefers tried to run after them, but they didn't know where to look. Violet and Noah had outwitted them.

"Violet," Noah called to his friend, hoping she was still running beside him. There was no reply.

Noah looked around the dense forest outside of their village. All he could see were green leaves. His entire body was still invisible. How could he see Violet if he couldn't even see himself?

"Violet!" he hollered, but again there was no reply. He worried that his shouting would alert the rainbow griefers to his location, and gave up calling out for her.

As Noah walked along a path, he took the remaining apple out of his inventory and took a bite. Once he settled by a tree, his hand became visible. The potion was losing its effect. When he was completely visible, he searched for Violet, but couldn't spot her anywhere. Noah took out his shears and cleared a path, hoping he would find Violet in the jungle.

As he walked toward the snowy Taiga Biome that was located beyond the jungle, he looked up and saw a familiar face.

"Violet!" He was so happy to be reunited with his friend.

"Hi Noah," Violet smiled.

Then Noah saw two people standing behind Violet, and realized she wasn't alone.

4

TEST FOR SURVIVAL

Violet introduced Noah to her new friends. "This is Ben and Hannah. They're from our village and want to join us in the fight against the griefers."

Noah wondered when Violet had had time to recruit the new people.

"Where did you meet them?" he asked Violet quietly, pulling her aside so Ben and Hannah were out of earshot.

"I found them hiding outside of town. They were both starving and had very little left in their food bars. When I offered them a potato, they told me how the rainbow griefers destroyed their lives." Violet walked Noah over to Ben and Hannah. "Please tell Noah what you told me."

Ben had tears in his eyes when he spoke of his wheat farm. "I had a very large and flourishing farm, but the rainbow griefers forbade me from eating any of my food. They said it was all for them. Every morning they would come by and gather all of my crops. Soon I was starving and had no resources to trade."

Hannah was shaking as she told her story. "I was an alchemist. When they found out that I brewed powerful potions, they forced me to live in a bedrock room and brew potions all day. There was no way to escape. They fed me very little and I was always weak. One day I decided I had had enough. I stopped making as many potions as they wanted. Daniel came to visit me. He informed me that I was being punished because I had slowed down my production. He said I wouldn't get food for the entire week. I saw he had left the door open, so I took my chance and threw a potion of harming on him, then fled out of the bedrock room. Now all the rainbow griefers are searching for me. They want revenge."

"Don't worry," Noah told Hannah, "they're searching for us too. We are all targets."

"If we band together, maybe all four of us can fight the rainbow griefers," suggested Violet.

Ben began to reminisce about the village before the rainbow griefers took over. "Remember how everyone from the town would have big parties and we'd all bring different food?"

"Yes." Hannah smiled. "It was so peaceful and everyone worked together to make it a beautiful place. I remember there was one person who could build the most unique buildings. People would come from all around the Overworld just to see the structures."

"That was Violet!" Noah blurted out.

"You were the famous builder?" Hannah looked at Violet, visibly impressed.

"Yes." Violet blushed. "But I don't build very much anymore. The griefers don't care about buildings, they just care about terrorizing people."

Noah looked at the sky. "It's not long before nightfall. We should make our way to the cold Taiga Biome. The rainbow griefers never travel that far, and they hate the snow because they can't blend in to the background. We can settle there and come up with a plan."

The group agreed with Noah and started to walk to the snow-covered biome. When they arrived, a wolf bolted past them.

"We need to build a shelter," said Ben.

"I can build an igloo," Violet suggested.

"Do we have enough time?" asked Ben, looking toward the setting sun.

"We have a world-famous builder here! She can do anything," Hannah proclaimed.

Violet laughed. "I can't do anything, but I'll try to build a quick igloo." Violet gathered the supplies to make the house from snow. "And you guys can help."

"I can't believe I'm helping you build," said Hannah, feeling a little like a star-struck fan.

"We all need to gather snow blocks," instructed Violet.

The group gave Violet blocks as she built the house as fast as she could. It started to snow just as Violet finished the first side of the house.

"I'm lighting a torch," Noah said. "It's too dark. Hostile mobs are going to spawn." But before Noah could even get the torch from his inventory, he spotted four vacant-eyed zombies off in the distance. The undead creatures silently crept through the snowy mountains, headed right in their direction.

"Zombies!" Hannah cried out. "We don't have any weapons. The rainbow griefers took everything from us. We are defenseless."

"What are we going to do?" Ben was worried this would be the end for him.

Violet tossed diamond armor and swords to her new friends. "Keep these. We are in this together. Once we defeat the rainbow griefers, you'll have all of your stuff returned to you. Life will go back to normal."

Ben and Hannah hoped Violet was right. They thanked her for the swords and armor and then sprinted toward the zombies, ready to defeat the hostile mobs of the night.

Violet started behind them, but Ben turned back and said, "No, Violet. Keep building the igloo with Noah. We'll handle this."

Noah helped Violet construct the walls of the igloo, then placed a torch on the wall by the front door. From the torch's light he could see Ben and Hannah battling with all their might. He cheered as they defeated the zombies and returned carrying the zombies' rotten flesh.

Another wolf sprinted past, and Ben leaned down, offering it the rotten flesh. The wolf smelled it and then took a bite, immediately tamed.

"Now we have a pet," he explained. Hannah wasn't sure Ben had made the best decision. They had a battle to focus on, and now they had to watch after a dog.

Violet approached the tamed wolf. "Can I name it?"

"Of course," Ben replied as he entered the half-finished igloo, the dog a few steps behind him.

"I want to call it Griefer," Violet joked.

"I think we should call it Hope," said Hannah.

The group stood around the dog in silence. They all nodded their heads in agreement.

In the pitch-black night sky, Hope watched as Violet put the roof on the house and finished the igloo.

5
ENCHANTING

When they were safely in the new igloo, bundled up underneath their red wool blankets, Violet told Hannah and Ben about the enchanted book she had found with Noah.

"Wow!" exclaimed Hannah. "That's going to come in very handy."

"Yes. In the morning we need to enchant our swords. They'll become so powerful, we'll be able to easily fight off rainbow griefers." Violet was excited.

As they wished each other goodnight, they all said how glad they were to have found each other, and they also admitted they were nervous about staging an attack on Daniel and his army.

"It's not going to be easy," remarked Hannah.

"Fighting for peace never is," said Violet, and the group went to bed.

When they woke up, they could see snow falling outside the igloo window. Violet rushed out to the white powder that covered the ground, squealing, "I want to play!"

Noah reminded her, "We have no time for playing. We have to enchant our swords and armor. Where's the anvil?"

Violet looked in a chest she had placed beside her bed, opening it to get the anvil. "Noah! It's gone!"

"What?" Noah was shocked.

"I had placed a chest in the corner and left it in there. It's gone and so are the extra diamonds I had stored." Violet was in tears. She regretted taking the items from her inventory and placing them in her chest. It was a dangerous thing to do, but she trusted everyone in the igloo.

Noah looked at the empty beds, "Where's Ben and Hannah?"

Violet couldn't believe they were missing. "They were thieves. They must have left with our stuff."

"How could they do that? And after all the stories they told us about the rainbow griefers," said Noah.

"This is a good lesson. We can't trust anyone." As those words flew from Violet's mouth, Ben and Hannah walked through the door. They were suited up in their armor.

"We have the anvil set up," said Hannah. "Do you have the enchanted book?"

"Why did you take my anvil without asking me?" Violet questioned them.

"I'm sorry, we thought we were being helpful. We just set it up outside next to the crafting table." Hannah led them to the front door. The anvil and table were set up underneath a covered patch of land outside the house.

"We thought you stole it," said Noah.

"Why would we do that?" Hannah was upset.

"Do you think we're thieves?" Ben hated when people didn't trust him.

"Well, you went through my chest without asking. When we woke up, you were missing and so was our stuff. What were we supposed to think?" Violet shouted in defense.

Hannah paused. She realized how their disappearance might have looked to Violet and Noah, and apologized.

Ben looked at the others and said, "I think we have to make a vow to trust each other. If we don't, this plan isn't going to work. I promise that I will stand by all of you during this war on the griefers."

The rest of the gang agreed, then walked outside into the snowy day and began to enchant their armor and swords with the enchanted book.

When they finished, Violet looked at her sword. "Although I don't want to battle a griefer right now, I really want to test this sword out."

The snow was getting thicker, hiding the sun, when an arrow seeming to appear out of nowhere hit Hannah. Luckily she wasn't hurt, because she was wearing armor.

"Is it a rainbow griefer?" Noah looked out in the distance.

"They never travel to the cold Taiga Biome," Violet reminded him. "It must be a hostile mob. They can spawn now, because the sun is being covered by the falling snow."

The group couldn't see anything. They wanted to ignore the stray arrow, but knew they couldn't for long.

"I think I see something moving over there." Noah pointed to a mountain covered with snow.

"Really?" Violet stood and stared, but didn't see anything.

"Stand still," Noah instructed. "If you just stand still, you can see something move."

"I see it!" Hannah shouted out. "It's a skeleton. It's so hard to see because it's camouflaged in the snow."

Hope barked as the skeleton moved closer to the group.

"There are two of them," Violet said as an arrow flew in her direction.

Violet was the only one in the group with a bow and arrow; she took it out of her inventory and aimed for the skeleton, but missed. "We're going to have to attack it with our swords."

"You were the one who wanted to try out our new swords," said Noah as he sprinted toward the bony skeleton with his enchanted diamond sword. With one swift blow, he destroyed the skeleton.

"Pick up his bow!" Violet shouted to Noah. "We only have one."

Hannah struck the other skeleton and destroyed it, retrieving its dropped bow and placing it in her inventory. She looked down at the diamond sword that had destroyed the skeleton. "Wow, these are powerful swords. No wonder Daniel is so upset that you have this enchanted book."

"Imagine what the griefers would do if they had this book? They would cause even more damage and destruction," Noah worried.

The group felt confident after defeating the skeletons, but they also knew they had a lot of work ahead of them. They had to come up with a strategy to defeat the griefers.

Then Violet lunged into a pile of snow.

"I told you we can't play now." Noah was upset with his friend. She was usually a lot more serious and focused.

"I'm not playing," Violet said as she made snowballs and began to pile them around her.

"Really? You're not playing? Because it looks like you're preparing for an epic snowball fight."

"No, come help me," Violet said as she placed the snowballs in her inventory. "I'm trying to stock up on weapons."

"That's right. Snowballs come in very handy when battling mobs in the Nether," remarked Hannah as she placed snowballs in her inventory.

"We aren't going to the Nether . . . are we?" Noah's voice quivered. He had never been to the Nether and heard it was a horrible place filled with lava and hostile mobs that shot fireballs at you.

"You Nether know," Ben joked.

"That's not funny," Violet said, "but we have to be prepared for everything. Now we need at least one more bow and some arrows so we have enough supplies to have a fair chance when we battle the griefers."

An arrow flew through the sky and landed near Hannah.

"I guess we know where we'll find the fourth bow," Hannah said as she charged toward the skeleton.

6

BATTLE FOR THE BOOK

The group had snowballs and bows and arrows, but they didn't have a plan. Violet wondered how long she and her friends would stay in the cold Taiga Biome before they had to head back to the village.

"I bet Daniel is going to send griefers to Taiga Biome," she told the others.

"Even if he doesn't, we have to head back. I can't imagine the damage he is doing. We have to stop him." Ben was ready for battle.

Before they went any further with a plan, they spotted colorful men sprinting past the birch trees.

"Do you think they see us?" Noah whispered to his friends.

"No, or they would have shot at us." Violet hid behind a tree. "We have to make our way back to shelter without them spotting us."

The group quietly trekked back to the igloo. When they were safely inside, Noah said in a panicked voice,

"It's just a matter of time before they discover this igloo. We're all doomed!"

"Noah, please." Violet paced the length of the living room. "I knew Daniel would send men looking for us. He really wants that book. We have to hide it."

"I bet he thinks only you and Noah are hiding out here. If Hannah and I hide, we can stage a sneak attack on the griefers." Ben was trying to plot a successful strategy.

They heard a noise and suddenly one of the rainbow griefers was ripping the door off the igloo. "We don't have any time to make plans. Whatever they do, I will deny having the book in my inventory," said Violet.

"I wonder who is in here." The griefer laughed and walked in to the living room. Noah and Violet stood with their diamond swords.

"Swords and armor aren't going to help you. Daniel has too many people after you," the colorful blue and red griefer jeered.

A pink and purple griefer appeared at the door. "Just hand over the enchanted book you stole from Daniel, and we will leave you alone. You can live in this cold dreary world forever. Just don't come back to the village."

Violet knew they weren't telling the truth. She had handed over valuables to the griefers before and they still attacked her. Violet was surprised when she heard Noah speak.

"We don't have the enchanted book. Somebody stole it from us," Noah told the griefers.

"You're lying," the red and blue griefer said as he held a diamond sword against Noah's throat.

"No, I'm not. Do you want to check? We kept it in a chest in our bedroom. It's empty now. We met a few people on the way here and they stole a bunch of stuff from us," Noah told them calmly, despite having a sword pointed at him.

"Go check the bedroom," the blue and red griefer ordered.

"Why do I have to look in the chest?" complained the pink and purple griefer.

"Because I said so." The blue and red griefer was annoyed.

The pink and purple griefer reluctantly moved across the living room. "You make me do everything."

As the pink and purple griefer walked into the bedroom, Hannah and Ben leapt at him with their swords. The griefer cried out and tried to fight back, but their powerful enchanted swords destroyed him.

At the same time, Violet and Noah lunged at the griefer that stood in their living room. They defeated him quickly, but not quickly enough. Noah was struck by the griefer's sword before he was destroyed.

"Are you okay?" Violet asked her friend.

"I'm very weak," Noah replied faintly.

Hannah and Ben walked into the living room. Hannah handed Noah some milk and he drank it slowly and began to feel better.

"Well, that worked well." Hannah was proud of another small victory.

"This is just the first of many griefer battles. We can't stay here. Daniel is going to keep sending griefers to find us. And we can't help anyone from here." Violet paced around the living room.

"That's right, we have to head back to the village. It's the only way we can actually help change things," Ben agreed with Violet.

"When I was trapped in the bedrock room making potions, I was actually being held in Daniel's palace, and I have an idea how we can get to Daniel and defeat him," said Hannah, slowly.

"That's great!" exclaimed Noah.

Violet said, "I built that palace. It wasn't always Daniel's. He stole it from a friend of mine."

"Then you probably know the inside of the palace better than I do. I spent most of my time trapped in the bedrock room."

"There weren't bedrock rooms when I built it. I bet Daniel added all sorts of sinister additions to that house," said Violet, "but I do have a good idea of the overall layout."

"We have to head to Daniel's palace," announced Ben.

Noah hoped his friends couldn't hear his heart beating as they sprinted back toward the village and straight for Daniel's palace.

7
STORMING THE PALACE

The group hurried into the village with Hope trailing behind them. Violet looked up into the trees and couldn't spot her tree house. It was gone.

"Noah," she cried, "they destroyed my tree house too."

"Oh no." Noah looked miserable.

"We have to hide," Hannah warned, as an army of rainbow griefers came marching through the village.

The group hid behind a tree. The rainbow griefers marched in a line, chanting a steady, deafening song. "We are powerful and strong. Nobody stands in our way," their voices boomed. Townspeople ran in terror. Violet watched as a rainbow griefer ripped an apple from a person's hands. She wanted to rush to the person and help them, but she knew it was best to hide. They needed to figure out their plan of action and stage an attack that would destroy these monsters and rid them from the town for good.

When the last rainbow griefer was no longer in sight, Noah said, "We need to get to the palace."

The grand palace stood just across from their hiding place. The entrance had two large columns and marble steps leading to the door.

"Are we going to enter through the front door?" asked Ben.

"I don't think that's a good idea," replied Violet. "Hannah, where were those secret tunnels?"

Hannah looked at the palace. She tried to remember how she escaped from the bedrock room. "I think the tunnel exit is right behind that tree with the flag."

Right outside the palace, there was a large oak tree where Daniel had placed a flag that read: RAINBOW PALACE. KEEP OUT.

Violet squinted her eyes at the ground behind the tree. "You're right—I think I see a hole. But it's still too far away, so I am not one hundred percent sure. We have to go investigate."

Hope began to bark.

"Oh no, this dog is going to give us away. What should we do?" Hannah was nervous.

Ben told the dog to stay, and Hope began to whimper. Ben had tears in his eyes when he said, "Hope, you're going to have to stay here. It's too dangerous for you in that palace. Stay here and protect my town."

Hope's tail wagged as he sat.

"We need to go to the palace now," instructed Ben.

"How are we going to do that?" Noah asked.

"Here." Hannah splashed a potion of invisibility on the group. "This is the last bottle I have, so we have to hurry."

The gang sprinted toward the hole behind the tree. Since they were invisible, nobody was able to see Ben look back at Hope. He wasn't sure he'd see his dog again, but he hoped he would. As he raced toward the palace, he heard Violet shout.

"It's here!" Violet crawled into the hole and the others followed.

The group found themselves in a dark tunnel. A creeper was floating in the distance. Violet was about to take out a bow and arrow to destroy it, but realized the explosion might alert the rainbow griefers to their presence. "Guys," Violet said in a soft whisper, "just hide from the creeper. We don't want it exploding."

The group walked in the opposite direction from the green, fiery, hostile creature. The bedrock hallway had a series of doors along the wall.

"Should we open one?" asked Noah.

"I bet they are jail cells, like the one I was kept in," Hannah said as she passed the closed doors.

Violet could make out a faint cry.

"Help!" a voice called out from behind one of the closed doors.

"Do you hear that?" Violet asked the others.

"I'm trapped. Help me!" the voice cried a bit louder.

"Yes, it's coming from behind the door." As Noah spoke, he could see his arm.

"Oh no," Hannah's voice shook. "The potion is wearing off. And I don't have any more left. Now the rainbow griefers will be able to find us."

"Calm down." Violet grabbed her armor out of her inventory and suited up. "We have to protect ourselves. Get your weapons out."

"I can hear someone coming." Violet looked down the hall.

Kaboom!

A rainbow griefer exploded with the creeper.

"We have to run," Ben told them.

"No, we have to help the person who is trapped behind this door. I know how it feels. I was once trapped in this palace and it's awful." Hannah opened the door.

A woman wearing a green helmet was hiding in the corner. "Who are you?" she called out. "Are you going to harm me?"

"No, come with us! Quickly, we have to go!" Violet called back.

"How do I know you aren't bad?" asked the woman.

"You're just going to have to trust us," Ben shouted, as the gang sprinted down the hall and away from the rainbow griefers that had gotten too close.

The woman with the green helmet followed the gang toward a large room at the end of the hall.

"It looks like we're trapped." Noah banged his pickaxe against the bedrock wall, but it didn't even make a dent.

"There has to be a way out of here." Violet looked down the hall. "I think if we go back, I saw another tunnel we could take."

Noah looked up and saw light. "Look!" he called out happily. "We can crawl through that hole."

"But we were just outside. We need to come up with a plan." Violet wanted to overthrow Daniel.

The woman wearing the green helmet looked at Violet. "Crawl through the hole. I have a plan."

"How do we know you're not going to harm us?" Noah asked her.

"You're just going to have to trust me," the woman with the helmet said, as three rainbow griefers came down the hall toward the group.

Noah, Violet, Ben, and Hannah followed the woman through the hole and into the sunny day.

The woman cried out as soon as she reached the surface, but it was too late.

Violet could see an army of rainbow griefers surrounding them.

One of the griefers smiled cruelly as he looked over Violet and her friends. "Daniel is waiting for you guys."

Another rainbow griefer looked at the woman in the green helmet, "Kyle, you can't escape. Daniel needs you to craft swords. We need to bring you back to your room."

The group was trapped. They followed the griefers back into the palace. This time they would be going through the front door.

8
STAYING ALIVE

Night began to set in before the group entered the palace, and a group of zombies made their way toward the palace door.

"Zombies," the head rainbow griefer called out to the pack. "We have to battle them, but don't let the prisoners escape."

"Don't worry, we have this covered. I don't even need to use a diamond sword," one of the warrior griefers boasted as he approached the hostile creatures of the night.

Violet was glad she didn't have to battle this hostile mob. Instead she watched the rainbow griefers lunge at the mass of zombies lumbering toward them.

The zombies were stronger than the rainbow griefers predicted. Two rainbow griefers were defeated.

"Wow, they aren't great fighters," said Kyle with scorn. "They forced me to craft swords all day, but they don't even know how to use them."

Another rainbow griefer was hurt. The head griefer looked over to the griefers that held Violet and her friends as prisoners.

"This is our chance." Noah and Violet's eyes met. "They need these guys to fight the zombies."

Violet leapt at the rainbow griefer in front of her, striking him with her diamond sword.

The griefers were shocked. Noah, Ben, Hannah, Kyle, and Violet used the opportunity to escape. They sprinted as fast as they could out of the town.

"Don't stop!" Violet called out when Hannah started to falter.

"We need to head back to the igloo," Noah decided.

"No, we need to go somewhere far away, where they won't find us. There we can work on a new plan." Violet took a deep breath as they continued running through the night.

"Stop!" Kyle yelled. "I've been hit by an arrow!"

"Skeletons!" Violet screamed, looking around for the bony creatures. But she couldn't see them anywhere.

"No!" Noah cried. "It's griefers!"

Two rainbow griefers were hiding behind a tree. Noah shot an arrow at one of them, but it bounced off his armor.

"Leave us alone," begged Violet. "We're far past the town limits. What do you want from us?"

"You think we only control just this town?" The rainbow griefer laughed. "Soon Daniel will control the entire Overworld."

The other rainbow griefer smirked. "You townspeople are so small-minded. You think this is the only town we have taken over? Yes, Daniel is in your town, but he has taken over dozens of villages all over the Overworld. He is the most powerful in all this world."

"We know he's powerful," said Violet, "but can you let us go? We never tried to harm you."

"Liar!" shouted the rainbow griefer. "Do you think we don't know who you are? Violet the famous builder!"

Kyle looked over at Violet. "Wow, I remember touring your tree house."

"Stop talking, Kyle!" ordered the rainbow griefer. "Daniel is very upset that you escaped. He needs you back in the palace to craft swords."

"Please let us go," Violet begged the griefers.

"And you, the builder! You are a thief! You stole the enchanted book. Daniel wants that book back. Hand it over now," he demanded, pointing a sword at Violet.

"Daniel will never know you found us," continued Violet. "Is there anything we can give you in exchange for our freedom?"

"I love watching you beg," the blue-faced rainbow griefer laughed loudly.

Noah didn't warn the griefer, but a creeper was silently lurking behind him.

Kaboom! The griefer exploded. The remaining griefer was taken by surprise. Noah leapt at him with his diamond sword, striking him until he was destroyed.

"We need to get out of here. This forest is probably crawling with griefers by now," Noah called out as he sprinted through the green forest and toward the desert that lay in the distance.

It was still quite dark, and the group had to be very careful as they headed toward the sandy terrain.

"Be sure to look out for hostile mobs and griefers," Noah told them.

The sun began to rise.

"I guess that's one less thing that we have to worry about now," Violet said, as the sun shone brightly in the sky.

"Look what the daylight revealed." Ben stood at the entrance of a desert temple.

"We have to go in." Kyle was excited. "I've never been in a desert temple before. I bet there's treasure inside."

"I'm sure there is," said Violet. "That could be very helpful. We need to stockpile resources. This isn't going to be an easy war to win."

"Instead of wasting time treasure hunting in a temple, we need to come up with a plan to take over Daniel's palace," argued Hannah.

"You're right, we also need a plan," Violet agreed, "but we can't pass up this opportunity to restock our supplies first." She walked through the door to the desert temple.

"We need to stay alive," Noah said. He joined Violet in the temple, and the others followed.

"They usually keep the treasure on the ground floor," Violet explained as she led the group to a room that contained a block of blue clay.

"Isn't this room booby-trapped?" Kyle asked. "I heard that there's TNT here and that it'll explode if you take out the treasure."

"I think you're right, but I know a lot about booby traps. We just have to avoid the pressure plate," Violet told them, and then she unearthed the treasure chest.

"Open it!" Kyle was excited to see what was inside.

Violet opened the chest. "Diamonds!"

"I can craft swords out of them!" Kyle told the group.

"And we can use the enchanted book to enchant them," added Violet.

The group gathered up the diamonds and placed them in their inventories.

"I think I hear something," said Noah. His heart began to pound again.

9
THE VIEW

The group saw a flash of rainbow pass by them and began to run. They held onto the diamonds as they raced out of the desert temple and onto the sandy biome ground.

"I see a forest up ahead. Let's hide there," cried Violet.

"I have a great idea," Noah said as they entered the tree-filled forest. "Let's build a tree house and use it as a fort."

"That's brilliant, Noah." Violet smiled. "The rainbow griefers are so obsessed with moving ahead, they never look up. They'll never think to look for us in the trees."

"And we'll have an advantage from high above. We'll be able to see them coming. They can't hide, they're so bright," said Kyle.

The group gathered wood and helped Violet craft a tree house high atop the trees in the jungle.

As they built, they began to reminisce about the days before the griefers. "I don't understand why Daniel wants to take over the world with evil. It was so nice before the griefers invaded," said Kyle.

"What did you do before the invasion?" asked Noah.

"I was a farmer, but I was known for crafting extremely powerful swords. My husband and I made swords for people all around the Overworld. When Daniel found out, he separated us and forced us to make swords in a small bedrock room. He gave me hardly any food."

Hannah jumped in. "He did the same thing to me. Except I was making potions."

"I wonder how many other people he has trapped in his palace," said Violet.

"I want to find my husband, Will. He must be in one of those rooms." Kyle's eye's filled with tears.

"We'll find him," Violet reassured Kyle as she placed the final wooden board on the tree house.

"Thanks," said Kyle, quietly, and then she went inside the tree house.

"You did an amazing job." Noah looked out at the tree house's view. "I can see the palace from here."

The others joined him and looked toward the palace.

Ben said, "We have such a great view—we'll be able to study the griefers from here. We can see if they are on a schedule. Maybe there's a break when one set of griefers stops guarding and the other group begins that we can use to our advantage."

"Good call. This is the perfect spot to stage our attack." Noah watched Daniel's headquarters. He wished he could just fly right into the palace and take Daniel away forever. He didn't want this evil dictator destroying his town. He looked over the village, gazing on the familiar iron golem and the streets lined with shops. He scanned the waterfront with its sandy beach. Despite being taken over by an evil man and his army of rainbow griefers, the town was still beautiful. As he stood and stared, Noah vowed to destroy Daniel.

"Look below," Violet said in a quiet whisper.

The gang looked down to see rainbow griefers sprinting through the forest. The griefers stopped.

"We lost them," an orange griefer called out.

"Where can they be?" growled a green sparkly griefer.

"They must have run very fast," said the orange man.

The sparkly griefer walked over to the water. "They have that potion expert with them. Perhaps they used the potion for underwater breathing and are escaping by sea."

"Should we look for them?" asked the orange griefer.

"I don't have any potions left," the sparkly griefer grimaced, "and now that the potion expert is gone, we have no way of getting more. Daniel is outraged. He wants that potion expert back."

"Let's keep moving. If they're not in the water, they couldn't have gotten very far. And it's almost dark. We'll need to build a shelter soon," said the orange griefer. And so the colorful men moved on through the green leaves and the sun began to set.

Noah whispered, "Did you hear what they said? They don't have any more potions. We have to use that to our advantage."

"I can brew potions up here if you guys can lend me supplies," said Hannah.

"That's great—we can pool our resources together," Violet told the group.

"Once we have a bunch of potions brewed, we should try to get back to the palace and use them to defeat Daniel," said Ben.

"We need a better plan," Noah jumped in. "Yes, we have potions, but that's not enough. We need to be prepared this time."

As the five of them sat there thinking, the sky turned dark and night set in.

"I bet we're safe from hostile mobs up here." Kyle looked at the dark sky and saw a bat fly by.

"No, creepers climb up ladders," Violet explained as she crafted beds for the group, "but once the beds are finished we'll be safe."

The group worked together to finish the beds. As they climbed in, they heard an explosion in the distance.

"I bet that was the griefers. I bet they met another creeper," Violet said quietly.

As Noah tried to cozy up underneath the covers, he could hear something or someone on the ladder.

"What's that noise?" Noah's voice was shaking.

10
SURPRISE ATTACK

Violet rushed to the ladder. She leapt at the rainbow griefer making its way into their living room. With two strikes of her powerful sword, Violet clobbered the pink griefer.

"Good job!" Noah cheered, relieved.

"There are zombies at the bottom of the ladder. I need help!" Violet shouted. The rest of the group threw on their armor and raced to her aid.

"The griefer must have been running from the zombies," said Ben. "Luckily you destroyed him so quickly he didn't even realize we were here."

Noah shot an arrow at a zombie from the ladder, and jumped down to the ground below.

Thump! He jumped on the zombie and destroyed it.

The remaining two zombies were getting closer, but Violet and her friends outnumbered the undead creatures and quickly obliterated them.

Exhausted from the battle, the gang was finally able to get some sleep. When they awoke in the morning, they were all very hungry.

"I have a few apples," Kyle told them. "I had been saving them in my inventory, because I never knew when Daniel would feed me."

"He did the same thing to me!" Hannah told Kyle.

The group ate the apples and tried to get their strength back so they would be prepared to attack Daniel.

"Look." Noah was standing by the window that overlooked the town. "Daniel is leaving the palace!"

Daniel stood out among his men. He didn't look like his army. He wasn't colorful like the rainbow griefers. Daniel had flaming red hair and wore diamond armor.

"Where is he going?" Violet wondered aloud.

"It looks like they are marching in our direction." Hannah was shocked. "Do you think he's looking for us?"

"I don't know," Ben responded, "but this might be a good time to begin our attack."

"But there are so many of them." Kyle looked at the rainbow griefer army that marched in a single line. "How can we possibly defeat them?"

Noah had a plan. "I think we should let them pass, and when they are gone, we should storm the palace."

"But what will we do once we get into the palace?" asked Ben.

"First, we'll find my husband," Kyle blurted out.

"Yes, Kyle's right. First we will set the prisoners free. They can help us win this war. If Daniel thinks they are important and powerful enough to keep as prisoners, then we need them on our side," said Violet.

"Then we'll take over the palace and free the people of the town." Ben was excited to get back to their village. He also wanted to see his dog again and make sure he was okay.

The group stood silently in the tree house as they listened to the griefers passing below.

"I hope they don't look up," Kyle whispered as she stood there.

"Me too," Violet agreed quietly. Violet thought about the enchanted book that she kept in her inventory. She knew that Daniel would destroy her and steal the book.

The gang held their breath as the griefers slowly made their way through the thick leaves of the forest and toward the desert biome.

"They must think we traveled very far from here." Noah peeked from the window, watching the griefers walk past the house.

"Shh!" warned Violet. "If one griefer looks back and sees this tree house, we are all finished. We can't let our guards down until the griefers are out of sight."

The griefers continued their trek. The group watched their rainbow colors through the trees. They could hear Daniel shouting at his army, "Faster, men! Faster! We need to find those thieves and put an end to them."

"They are looking for us!" Violet said when the griefers were out of sight.

"It's time for us to head to the castle." Noah put on a brave face as he made his way down the ladder in his armor.

The gang followed. As the rainbow army searched the sandy desert, Violet and her friends were heading home. They were on a mission to restore peace to their once thriving village. Although all of their hearts beat loudly and they had no idea what they would encounter when they reached the palace, they knew this was a battle that must be fought.

The palace was in sight when arrows began to rain down on the gang.

"Looks like they left a bunch of griefers here to keep watch over the community."

"Don't worry," Noah said confidently. "We've got this."

Noah looked over at Hannah, and she reached for a potion of weakness to splash on the griefers that sprinted toward them.

"I can't move," a griefer shouted out.

"Me neither!" groaned another.

Noah led the group through the palace doors and down the stairs to free the prisoners.

"Will!" Kyle shouted as she ran down the hall in search of the room that contained her husband.

Noah opened each door, announcing to the prisoners, "We come in peace, but come with us!"

They were all grateful to be free and they followed Noah, the accidental warrior, through the halls of the palace.

11
HELPFUL HINTS

"**W**ill!" Kyle exclaimed when the door of the last room was opened. But it wasn't Will. There was a woman wearing a checkered shirt and a black helmet. She thanked them for setting her free, but tears filled Kyle's eyes.

"Are you okay?" the woman asked Kyle.

"I'm glad you're free," replied Kyle. "I just didn't find the person I was looking for."

Violet comforted Kyle. "We'll find your husband." But Violet wasn't sure she believed her own words.

"Everyone! Pay attention!" Noah addressed the freed prisoners gathered in the hallway. "We are taking over the palace and storming Daniel's room. Follow me."

Violet and her friends were shocked to hear someone call out, "Why? What has Daniel done to us?"

Noah couldn't believe anybody would ask this question. Daniel was the head of the griefers. He was the enemy.

"Daniel devastated our town," Violet shouted.

Many of the prisoners joined in. "Down with Daniel."

Daniel's defender, sporting a red jumpsuit and blue hair, called out, "Stop! Daniel gives us food every day and protects us from hostile mobs. Since I've been in that room, I haven't had to fight and I could just craft armor for him."

"But you don't have any freedom." Ben was angry.

"I never really left the village before! What's the difference if I'm in here?" she asked.

"He stopped us from seeing the sun and breathing fresh air. We don't ever get any breaks," one of the prisoners called out.

"He took me away from my family," shouted another.

"He is keeping my husband as prisoner," added Kyle.

Noah could hear footsteps in the distance. He looked at the woman in the red jumpsuit. "Stay here. It's your choice. But we have to go."

The prisoners followed Noah down the narrow hall and up the stairs. At the top of the stairs, in a room on the right, two orange griefers stood talking.

Noah hid tight against the wall and eavesdropped on their conversation.

"Daniel will be back soon. We better check on the prisoners." A griefer came out of the room and walked past Noah and toward the stairs, where all Noah's followers were waiting.

Noah took out his sword, readying himself for an attack.

But the griefer stopped short when the other griefer called out, "Daniel is on a quest to find the thieves who stole his book and to get the potion expert back. He won't be back for a long time. We can check on them later. I'm hungry. Let's go to the kitchen and eat some cake. You know how much Daniel hates when we eat cake. We never get any. Let's go get some now while he's gone."

"Good thinking," the first griefer replied.

Both griefers turned and walked toward the kitchen and away from the stairs. Noah gave a sigh of relief and signaled to the others, who quickly dashed into the room the griefers had left empty.

"The master suite is through there and over to the left," Violet called to them. "I assume that's where Daniel has set up his headquarters."

Noah sprinted in the direction she pointed, then halted and ordered everyone to stand back. "Um, I think you're right."

"Oh no!" Violet's eyes widened. There were at least forty rainbow griefers standing in front of the door to Daniel's room. "It's like a human rainbow!"

"What should we do?" asked Ben.

"Do you think I should splash a potion on them?" Hannah had a bunch of mixtures in her inventory, but she still lacked the potion of invisibility.

"I guess that's a good plan." Noah was at a loss.

Hannah bravely approached the griefers, surprising them as she splashed a potion of weakness on as many as she could at once. A group of griefers leaped at Hannah, and before anyone could come to her rescue, they overwhelmed her with their swords until she was destroyed.

The others raced to her side, but it was too late. Hannah was gone. In a moment of rage and with all of his energy, Noah lunged at the griefers with his sword, but even with his anger, he was too weak to win the battle. With one final hit from the griefer's sword, Noah, the accidental leader, was about to respawn in the tree house in the forest. The prisoners witnessed his destruction and quickly abandoned the palace.

Violet, Kyle, and Ben were left to battle the remaining griefers on their own. Luckily the effects of the potion hadn't worn off, so many of the griefers were weakened, but the battle was still uneven. Violet looked back in hope of support from any of the remaining freed prisoners, but they had all fled. Only one prisoner stayed behind. She was wearing a red jumpsuit and had her diamond sword pointed at Violet.

12
SPELLBOUND

Violet was surrounded. She was in a fierce battle with a purple griefer, and now she was about to be attacked by a prisoner she had freed.

"Stop!" Violet screamed to the prisoner, but the woman in the red jumpsuit didn't listen. She leapt forward and, to Violet's surprise, struck the rainbow griefer that was attacking her. With two fast blows, the woman obliterated the griefer.

"Thank you." Violet was shocked.

"There's no time to thank me." The prisoner grinned. "We have to battle these griefers."

Even with the additional help from the woman in the red jumpsuit, they were still outnumbered. Once the potion began to lose its potency, there were more soldiers to battle.

"We can do this!" Ben shouted to his friends, but he spoke too soon. The minute the words fell from his lips, another horde of griefers barreled down the hall, surprising him from behind. With Ben destroyed, there were only three people left to battle an army.

Kyle slammed her sword against an orange griefer who was eating a piece of cake, instantly destroying him. When the other griefers saw, they came together and turned their swords on her. As she tried to fight back, she saw an arrow strike one of the griefers that was hurting her. Before one final blow destroyed her, she thought she saw her husband Will in the corner of the palace. He was holding a bow and arrow.

"Will," she cried out, but she never heard the response. Within seconds she was respawning in the tree house.

Violet was the only one left. Griefers surrounded her, and she didn't even have time to surrender. The last thing she remembered was seeing a griefer open the door to Daniel's room. She wanted to peek inside but couldn't.

"Is everyone okay?" Violet asked as she respawned in the tree house.

"I'm glad the tree house is still here," said Ben, pacing back and forth. "I thought that griefer tipped Daniel off to our location, and assumed it would have been destroyed when we were in the palace." Ben was nervous, and wanted to help Noah and Violet come up with a new plan.

"It's almost nighttime," Violet told the battle-weary group. "We need to eat and sleep and regain our strength. We have a serious battle ahead of us tomorrow."

"Are we going back to the palace?" Hannah's voice shook.

"We have to go back," replied Kyle. "I saw Will in the palace. We have to help him."

"Yes, we have to save him and the town," agreed Violet. "We will go back and this time we'll have a better plan."

"We need a miracle," Ben called out.

Violet took the enchanted book out of her inventory and held it up for the group to see. As she leafed through the pages, she smiled. "No, we need a little magic."

She gathered all the diamond armor and used the book to enchant the armor to withstand fire.

She held up the flame-resistant armor and asked, "Does anybody have any TNT?"

The group searched through their inventories. "I have a lot of snowballs." Ben rifled through his things. "But only one block of TNT."

"I have a bunch." Noah counted. "Five blocks."

The others counted their blocks of TNT as Violet paced the length of the room, trying to come up with the details for a strong attack. She paused. "Does anybody know how to make the cube of destruction?"

"No," Kyle replied. "I thought that was just a myth. I didn't know that really existed."

"We're going to have to blow up the palace. We need to make sure we have enough explosives to actually destroy it," Violet informed the gang.

"But you spent such a long time building that palace." Noah remembered how much work Violet put into its construction. It was her first building project and she spent months designing it and acquiring all of the resources. There were massive, grand rooms to entertain in, elaborate bathrooms, twenty fireplaces in total, and four large terraces with views of the water.

"It doesn't matter anymore." Tears streamed down Violet's cheeks. "That was before the invasion, when life was different. We can always rebuild, but we'll never be able to create anything if Daniel is in charge. He has stolen everyone's freedom and power. I'd destroy anything I built to get our freedom back. Without that, we are nothing."

The sky turned pitch black.

"Oh no, we better get into our beds. We don't want to get attacked by hostile mobs." Ben looked out at the night sky, searching for the hostile mobs that might be making their way toward the tree house.

"Let's just hope that we can sleep through the night without a visit from the griefers." Violet climbed into her bed and pulled the wool blanket over her tired body.

Violet didn't tell the others that she had a hard time falling asleep. Her brain was racing with thoughts of the attack on the palace. She was trying to figure out the best places to put the TNT to optimize their power and create the most devastating destruction. She didn't want to leave any part of the palace intact.

13
DANIEL'S STORY

As the others slept, Violet heard voices below the tree house. She looked down. Zombies were attacking a group of griefers. They were safe from the zombies in the tree house, since the undead mob couldn't climb up the ladder. But Violet held her breath and hoped the griefers didn't discover the ladder. She had built the house in a thick patch of leaves, and the ladder was camouflaged with the tree bark, but that hadn't stopped the sole griefer from climbing up the night before.

The zombies were defeating the griefers. Violet couldn't believe her eyes. Zombies were an easy mob to defeat. These griefers weren't skilled fighters. Violet wondered how Daniel recruited his rainbow soldiers. They were probably very new to the world of Minecraft when he found them and convinced them to change their skin to rainbow and join his army. She wondered how he repaid them. Maybe he told them he would protect them from hostile mobs.

Violet thought back to the battle in the palace. The rainbow griefers weren't the best fighters. They were only powerful because there were so many of them and they were all very healthy. Daniel made sure to provide the rainbow griefers with enough food to give them plenty of lives. It took a lot of energy to battle a rainbow griefer.

The zombies wandered around below the tree house, fading as the sun rose. Violet's friends woke up.

"Did you get any sleep?" asked Noah.

Hannah walked over and handed Violet an apple.

Violet took a bite, and with a yawn replied, "No, I didn't get any sleep. I was too busy watching zombies battle rainbow griefers."

"Where are the griefers?" Ben looked below, but there was nobody beneath the tree house.

"The zombies defeated them." Violet chewed.

"What? They lost to zombies?" Hannah didn't believe her.

"Are you sure you weren't dreaming?" questioned Noah.

"No, I saw it. There were four blue griefers battling about seven zombies and—"

Noah interrupted her, "They won?!"

"Yes," Violet clarified, "and I realized a serious weakness of the griefer army. I believe many of them aren't truly skilled fighters."

"Why would he use bad fighters?" Kyle wasn't sure how Daniel could employ a useless army.

"Shh!" Hannah told them as she saw someone approach below. She waved for them to join her.

The others walked softly to the window.

"Why is he alone?" Violet whispered, watching Daniel walking in the forest.

Noah grabbed his bow. "Do you think I can hit him from here?"

"No!" Violet grabbed the bow from Noah's hands.

"What are you—crazy? I can do a sniper attack!" Noah didn't understand Violet's hesitation.

"What if you miss? We don't want him to know our hiding place. We have to fight him on the ground."

Wearing armor and carrying swords, the friends descended the ladder and sprinted toward Daniel in a surprise attack.

"I knew I'd find you here," Daniel said calmly. "Please stop—don't fight me. I will only respawn and find you again, so there's no point. I can offer a better alternative."

"We have no interest in hearing your plans. We want you to leave this town and leave us in peace." Noah pointed his diamond sword at Daniel.

"You should join the rainbow griefers. I will make you the most powerful men in my army."

"Never!" Violet shouted.

"Look at you, Violet, so determined to save your village. It's a losing battle. You'll never free your town of us."

"Yes, we will." Ben stood next to Violet.

"Violet, you have convinced these poor people to follow you, but you know that in a few days you'll all be prisoners in my palace." Daniel shook his head.

"No, we won't!" Violet shouted.

"I see you have three of my prisoners in your make-shift army. They can tell you all about your future in a jail cell." Daniel smiled.

"Okay, capture me," taunted Violet.

"I don't want to capture you. I want you to join me. If you come now, I promise no one will harm you."

"Being a part of your army is harmful," Noah called out.

"My army isn't harmful. And everyone here is quite useful to me. I want you to join me." Daniel approached Violet. "You also have something I need. You stole my book. That was my secret treasure. You are a thief. You're lucky you're not in jail."

"Me? You stole from everyone in this town," replied Violet.

"No, I've improved this town. I'm going to help the Overworld. We keep order and help people survive hostile mob attacks."

"You force people to cater to all of your needs. You destroy towns and control them with violence. Ever since you took over this town, I haven't been able to build anything."

"Violet, if you join my army, I'll let you build all over the Overworld. I can have you construct palaces for me in every biome. You will become the most world-renowned builder in all the Overworld."

"I would never build anything for you." Violet rushed forward and struck Daniel with her sword.

A sea of colorful griefers emerged from the leaves and descended upon the group.

"It's a trap!" Ben shouted.

Hundreds of rainbow griefers flooded the forest. There was nowhere to run and nowhere to hide.

"You should have joined my army when you had the chance," Daniel laughed as he watched his army battle Violet and her friends.

Violet used every bit of energy to battle these evil griefers. She knew they weren't skilled. Hannah emptied her inventory of potions, splashing as many as she could at the enormous army.

"Yes!" Hannah called out when she realized she did have one potion of invisibility bottle left among her liquids. She splashed it on her friends and screamed, "Sprint!"

As they raced through the leafy forest, Violet heard Daniel shout, "Where did they go?" He was dumbfounded.

The gang didn't stop until they were beside the ocean and the potion was wearing off. They could see their hands. Once they were fully visible, Violet took a deep breath and asked, "Does everyone still have their TNT blocks?"

14
POTIONS AND PORTALS

"I don't think we're safe." Violet could hear footsteps. "In minutes, Daniel's army will be here."

"Oh no!" Ben called out. "I think they're here now."

A red body rushed through the leaves. Noah shot an arrow, but the voice called out weakly, "Don't shoot!"

"It's the woman from the palace," exclaimed Violet.

The woman wearing the red jumpsuit emerged from the leaves. "Daniel and his army are on their way and they have seriously bad plans for you. You won't just be kept as prisoners. He is going to do something sinister."

"What? Did you overhear anything?" asked Noah.

"I couldn't hear everything, but it was something about switching you guys to hardcore mode and forcing you to destroy each other."

Violet gasped. "That's horrible."

"I know. I'm sorry I ever doubted you," said the woman. "But you have to go, and fast."

Violet began to place blocks of obsidian on the ground.

"What are you doing?" asked Noah.

"We have to go to the Nether. There's no way out." Violet ignited the obsidian portal.

The group stood on the platform, but the woman with the red jumpsuit remained behind.

"Do you want to join us?" Violet asked quickly before the portal closed.

"No, I'll stay here. When Daniel comes, I'll tell him you're under the water looking for Ocean Monuments. He thinks I'm on his side." She smiled through the purple mist.

"Should we trust her?" Noah asked as they resurfaced by a lava waterfall.

"I guess we'll find out if she's trustworthy if Daniel follows us to the Nether," replied Violet as she tried to get her bearings in their new surroundings.

The only person who was happy to be in the Nether was Hannah. "I can gather materials to brew potions while we're here! That will help us."

A ghast flew from the sky, shooting a powerful fireball at Hannah. She jumped back and narrowly avoided the blast. The white ghast flew closer and shot another fireball.

"Get your snowballs out," instructed Noah.

The gang threw cold snowballs at the hot ghast, quickly destroying both the fireball and the evil creature.

"The Nether is filled with all sorts of destructive mobs," said Kyle, looking at the lava-filled landscape with dread.

"Yes, but we have a lot of snowballs, so we should be fine," reassured Violet.

The group explored, looking for Nether wart and soul sand for Hannah's potions.

"Guys!" Hannah called out. "I think I see a Nether fortress in the distance."

"You do!" Noah was excited. "Look, it's just beyond that lava waterfall."

As the group walked toward the grand fortress, Violet reminded them, "We have to stay focused. We need to find a way back into Daniel's palace. We have to destroy it. Losing the palace will seriously weaken him, and it's our only hope of regaining our freedom."

"Look out!" warned Ben.

Four blazes flew through the sky, aimed at the group.

"Snowballs!" shouted Noah.

The group blasted the blazes with snowballs. As the final blaze was destroyed, Noah checked his inventory. "I am running low on snowballs. How about you guys?"

The others were also low, leaving them at a clear disadvantage in the Nether.

Violet reminded Hannah to pick up the blaze rods that the blazes had dropped when they were destroyed. "You can use that to brew potions."

"Thanks," said Hannah, placing the rods in her inventory.

"The Nether fortress is just steps away. Let's go in, get the Nether wart, and then head back to the Overworld. We need to stage our attack," demanded Violet.

The group walked into the Nether fortress. Kyle looked at the staircase with Nether wart growing from its side and commented, "Although this place is dark and creepy, there is something beautiful about it."

"I agree," Hannah said as she gathered the Nether wart and placed it in her inventory.

As Violet explored, she noticed the reddish walls glowing. "It's glowstone!"

Noah banged his pickaxe against the temple wall, picking up the blocks of the rare glowstone.

"We have to get going," Violet demanded.

"I don't think we're going anywhere," Kyle stuttered as she pointed at three Wither skeletons coming straight for them.

Violet leapt at them with her diamond sword, but before she could attack, one of the black skeletons struck her hard.

Noah and Ben rushed to join Violet in battle. They struck the bony creatures until they were destroyed and dropped Wither skulls on the ground.

"The battle isn't over!" cried Hannah.

"I don't see any more Wither skeletons," replied Violet.

"Look down!" Hannah lunged at a magma cube, splitting it into smaller cubes, which the group struck with their enchanted diamond swords.

"This place is a death trap," Violet proclaimed as more magma cubes spawned around them.

"There must be a magma cube spawner in the fortress! We have to find it!" Noah searched the fortress, but couldn't find the spawning room. Violet joined Noah on his search while the others skillfully battled the magma cubes.

"Watch out!" Violet shouted to Noah, who was inches from a lava well. "Don't fall in!"

The duo raced through the structure until they came upon the treasure hidden in every Nether fortress.

"We should unearth this treasure," said Noah, walking up to the chest and opening it.

"Flint and steel! How useful!" Violet placed the flint and steel in her inventory as Noah moved on to explore the fortress further.

"Look what I found," he called back to Violet.

She raced to him and lit a torch in the room where he stood. They had found the magma cube spawner; now they had to work fast to deactivate it.

"We need lava!" Noah sprinted to the well and filled a bucket with lava. Violet followed, filling a bucket of her own.

They had to be very careful as they extracted the lava, because it was very harmful and they could be destroyed. Violet especially didn't want to respawn in the tree house, because she was worried that by now it would be filled with rainbow griefers.

"Throw it on the spawner," instructed Noah.

Together Noah and Violet flooded the spawner with lava, then raced to the main room to help the others battle the remaining magma cubes. As they entered the battle, they struck as many small cubes as they could. The room was filled with the tiny magma cubes. Hannah picked up the magma cream each cube dropped when it was destroyed. When the final cube was gone, the group let out a collective sigh of relief.

"Violet and I found treasure," Noah told the group.

The gang was excited.

"Did you find gold ingots?" asked Kyle.

"Did you find diamonds?" questioned Hannah.

"No, but we have flint and steel, which will come in very handy when we head back to the Overworld and stage our attack," Violet informed the group.

"I think the plan to blow up the palace is terrific, but how are we going to get into the palace carrying bricks of TNT? It doesn't seem realistic. They will attack us before we even get through the door." Kyle was confused; she liked Violet's idea, but didn't think the execution was fully developed.

Violet's eyes lit up. "Don't worry, I have the best plan!"

15
BURNING DOWN THE HOUSE

"**W**e have to change our skins," Violet said as they stood in the fiery Nether fortress.

"What?" Hannah was confused.

"We need to become rainbow," explained Violet, "so they'll think we're part of their army and we can stage a sneak attack."

"Speaking of a sneak attack!" Noah jumped as four yellow blazes flew in their direction.

One of the fireballs struck Kyle and Hannah, instantly destroying them.

"Oh no!" Violet threw a snowball at the blaze, but she wasn't fast enough and was the next to be hit by the fiery blast.

Noah and Ben were left to defeat the blazes on their own. When six more shot through the sky, they knew it was an impossible fight. Even with an inventory full of snowballs, they were going to be destroyed. They gathered all of their energy to battle the flaming mob, but it was a losing battle. Both Noah and Ben were destroyed.

When Violet respawned in the tree house, she was relived to find it intact. Her fears of rainbow griefers taking over the home were unfounded. They were safe and could stage their attack on the palace.

"Is everyone okay?" asked Violet as her friends began to respawn in their beds.

There was a collective response ranging from "Yes, I'm okay," to "Wow, that was a crazy trip to the Nether." Everyone was relieved the tree house was still there.

Violet discussed her plan of changing skins and asked everyone, "What color do you want to be? I think I want to be pink."

"Are you sure this is a good idea?" Noah questioned nervously.

"Yes, it's the only way we can get into the palace," Violet defended her plan. "Now we have to choose new rainbow skin and we have to do it fast."

The group chose various colors. Violet was shocked to see Noah change from his usual black helmet and diamond armor to a bright sparkly purple.

"It's so strange to see us this way." Ben looked at his new green arm.

Hannah worried, "I hope this works out. I'm really nervous."

"We have to do this, Hannah," said Violet. "We don't have any choice; it's the only plan that might work."

"We should go now, before night sets in," Noah said as he climbed down the ladder. The others followed him, and the newly minted fake rainbow people walked through the forest toward their old town.

"Do we agree on where we should place the TNT?" asked Violet.

"Yes, we should leave blocks all around the palace to maximize the destruction." Noah rattled off a list of locations.

"That's the entire palace," said Ben. "How are we going to casually place TNT blocks around the palace and then ignite them?"

"We're going to have to separate. We each take some blocks, ignite them, and then run. Each brick of TNT should be placed by a window or a door, so we have an easy escape," Violet told them.

The palace was just in sight and Noah felt a lump in his throat. "I hope this works."

"It will. I'm telling you, I know it will," Violet said with confidence.

"Famous last words," joked Ben.

"This isn't the time for jokes or doubt." Hannah was annoyed. "It's time for action. And we need to get this right."

"We're almost there. Since there are five of us, four should each take a corner of the building and one can take the entrance. Let's look at our clocks, and at half day we will all set off the TNT and sprint out of the palace. We meet up at the tree house." Violet looked at her friends and hoped this plan would work.

They each went their separate ways heading toward the palace. Violet chose the entrance, because she assumed that was the trickiest to blow up, and since she came up with the plan, she believed it was her responsibility to take the riskiest part.

As Violet walked toward the palace steps, she was greeted by a purple rainbow griefer. She smiled at the griefer and he smiled back. It was so strange to feel at peace in her old town. It was also odd to be wearing rainbow griefer skin.

A townsperson walked by and the purple rainbow griefer lunged at him, demanding an apple. The townsperson cowered as he took an apple from his inventory and handed it to the rainbow griefer.

The purple griefer insisted, "I want another one for my friend."

Violet shuddered when she heard the word friend. She wanted to refuse the apple, but she didn't want to give herself away. She took the apple and placed it in her inventory. She promised herself that she would return it when the war was over.

But she was wasting time, and Violet knew she had to act fast. She had seconds to ignite the block of TNT. She sprinted toward the doorway. The purple griefer was suspicious and trailed behind her.

"What are you doing?" the purple griefer questioned as Violet hid behind the pillar that stood in the entrance of the grand palace.

"Daniel asked me to fix something," Violet replied.

"Pink griefers don't fix things. Only green and orange griefers fix stuff. You aren't telling the truth," the purple griefer shouted. "I'm reporting you."

Before the purple griefer got any closer, Violet ignited the TNT and ran as fast as she could toward the tree house. She looked back and didn't see or hear any explosions. She hoped she wasn't off with her timing.

"Oh no!" she worried. "I hope my friends are okay."

Kaboom!

She paused and looked back to see a series of explosions. The palace was destroyed. She hoped for the best as she dashed through the dense forest and climbed the ladder to the tree house.

When Violet reached the final rung, she heard a familiar voice. "You think you're going to get away with this?"

She was alone in the tree house with Daniel.

16
FACTS OVER FICTION

"I thought you were Violet and her makeshift army," Daniel said, not realizing that Violet was disguised as a rainbow griefer.

"They blew up your palace." Violet tried to sound angry.

"They will pay for it. Don't worry—I have a plan." He looked out at the palace. "They won't get away with this."

"No, they won't." She hoped Daniel couldn't hear her heart pounding. She didn't want to get caught and was very nervous.

"They'll show up here soon. They have no other place to go." Daniel paced as he waited for Violet and her friends.

"I think I hear someone coming up the ladder." Violet rushed to the ladder to signal to her friends that Daniel was there. But she was too late and a rainbow griefer climbed into the tree house.

Violet looked at the griefer. None of her friends chose orange. This was an actual griefer.

"Daniel, I have serious news," the orange griefer announced. "The townspeople who stole your enchanted book have changed their skins."

"What are you talking about? What do you mean changed their skins?" demanded Daniel with a raised voice.

"They are posing as rainbow griefers," the orange griefer told Daniel.

Violet's heart beat even louder. She felt her throat close. She tried to take a deep breath as she walked toward the stairs.

"Stop," Daniel ordered Violet.

"What?" She tried to appear calm.

"You need to help me," said Daniel. "I didn't tell you that you could leave."

Violet relaxed. Daniel didn't realize that she was the enemy. But she worried what would happen when her friends finally showed up.

"Do you know what colors these people chose as their skins?" Daniel questioned the orange griefer.

"I'm not sure. I just heard that rainbow griefers blew up the palace. I knew that one of your soldiers would never do something that terrible, and I realized it must be the revolting townspeople." As the orange griefer spoke, he looked at Violet.

Violet hoped he didn't suspect her. She shook her head as the orange griefer spoke to show him that she agreed with him.

"We need to get out of the tree house. It's obvious that they aren't returning here. And they must have survived the attack, because none of them have respawned in their beds." Daniel walked toward the stairs. "Follow me."

He reached the first rung of the ladder when Hannah began to respawn on the bed. Daniel sprinted back into the tree house and pointed his diamond sword at Hannah.

"You are going to pay! You're an imposter. How dare you dress up as a rainbow griefer and destroy my palace." Daniel struck her with his diamond sword.

"Men," Daniel called out to Violet and the orange griefer, "destroy her! And then reset her to hardcore mode and get rid of her properly." Daniel laughed as he dictated those orders.

Hannah looked up to see Violet. She was confused. Hannah hoped Violet didn't join Daniel. Violet tried to smile at Hannah to signal that it was okay, but Hannah didn't notice. She was terrified of being placed on hardcore.

Daniel descended the ladder, leaving his two soldiers to destroy Hannah. The orange griefer struck Hannah, but she fought back.

"Aren't you going to help?" the orange griefer asked Violet. "What are you, lazy?"

"No!" Violet struck the orange griefer with her sword.

"What are you doing?" the griefer shouted.

Violet didn't reply, she just delivered a final blow that destroyed the orange griefer.

It wasn't long before night would set in. Violet and Hannah's friends hadn't returned, and it was no longer safe for them to stay at the tree house. They reluctantly made their way down the ladder. They looked for Daniel or any other rainbow griefers that might be lurking in the forest, but it was empty. It was an eerie and silent landscape as the two searched for their friends.

"We need to go back to the town and find them," Violet told Hannah. "They know we are dressed as rainbow griefers. Our friends aren't safe. They're probably being kept prisoner."

Hannah replied, "I wonder where they keep prisoners now that we have destroyed the palace."

A familiar voice called out from a patch of leaves, "You don't want to know. It's awful."

The woman with the red jumpsuit appeared in front of them. "I'm sorry. I didn't realize you were part of Daniel's army." Her voice shook.

"No, it's us. The people who asked you to join us in the Nether portal," Violet announced.

"But you're rainbow."

"We're in disguise," Hannah replied.

"We need to save our friends," Violet said. "Where is the prison?"

"I know they have a second prison. It's at an old wheat farm right by the palace. It's a very evil place run by a mean green griefer named Wade. He stole the wheat farm from a man named Steve."

"I bet that's where they are keeping our friends!" Violet cried. "Lead us there."

The woman in the red jumpsuit led Violet and Hannah toward the village and past the destroyed palace. As they made their way to the wheat farm, the sun began to set.

Two Endermen carrying blocks walked past. Although the group tried not to stare, one of the Endermen shrieked and teleported toward them.

Violet struck him with her diamond sword, but it made no impact. Hannah splashed a potion of harming at the Endermen, destroying the menacing mobs. They dropped Ender Pearls as they disappeared, which Violet picked up and placed in her inventory.

As night closed in, zombies began to invade the town, ripping doors from their hinges. Townspeople emerged from their homes when they realized the rainbow griefers weren't going to fight off the zombies. Too busy searching for Hannah and Violet, the griefers had left the towns-people to battle the zombies alone.

The weakened townspeople tried to fight the zombie invasion. Hannah, Violet, and the woman in the red jumpsuit joined the townspeople in the zombie battle, striking them with their swords. As Violet delivered a fatal blow to a zombie, she realized that she had to end this battle. She must free her friends. She worried that they had already been set on hardcore mode and forced to destroy each other. If that happened, they'd never respawn. They would be gone for good. She wanted to help the townspeople fight, but she had bigger battles to conquer.

Violet and Hannah followed the woman in the red jumpsuit through the town and to the wheat farm. She could hear someone call out, "Let the battle begin!"

Violet cringed. She hoped they weren't too late.

17
VILLAGERS

"This is it," the woman in the red jumpsuit told Violet and Hannah. "I have to go. If they find me, they will place me on hardcore and destroy me."

"They're ruthless." Violet was upset.

The woman shrugged. "You guys blend in here. I'd stand out and blow your cover."

Violet and Hannah walked into the wheat farm. Despite the evil that lurked on the farm, it was a jovial scene. Griefers stood laughing and cheering. Violet and Hannah tried to weave through the crowd to see what battle everybody was watching.

"What's going on?" Violet asked a rainbow griefer as she squeezed past.

"These traitors are battling each other in hardcore. The woman doesn't have much energy left. It won't be long," a blue griefer informed Violet.

Violet pushed her way to the front. The griefers had set up a stage and two people were battling each other.

It's Kyle and Will! Hannah couldn't believe it.

Violet closed her eyes. It was too painful to watch.

"I have a plan. Don't worry," Hannah whispered to Violet.

Hannah approached Kyle and Will and splashed a potion of strength and healing on them.

"What are you doing?" one of the griefers shouted.

"She isn't one of us. She's one of the missing traitors. Wade! Capture her!" a purple griefer exclaimed.

The orange griefer named Wade grabbed Hannah. Violet rushed toward Kyle and Will, shouting, "Guys, we have to save Hannah."

The trio attacked the rainbow griefer that held Hannah. Everything stopped when a loud voice boomed through the wheat farm. "*Stop*," it demanded.

Everyone looked back to see Daniel standing by the entrance. "Looks like I have all of my traitors here. Good job, boys. Let's destroy them all at once. Set them to hardcore mode."

A horde of griefers stormed through the crowd and captured Violet and her friends. Violet shook nervously. There was no way out. She had no backup because all of her friends were captured.

"Game over." She looked at Hannah.

"There has to be something we can do," Hannah replied.

"We're outnumbered. We tried." Even though she was happy to see Noah and the others, Violet was sad they had failed.

"I'm sorry," she said to her friends.

"It's not your fault," said Noah.

Daniel approached the group with a huge grin. "Looks like this is the end," he laughed.

Violet looked up in shock. Then replied, "Maybe not."

Daniel turned around and was stunned. The woman in the red jumpsuit entered, accompanied by all the prisoners Violet and her friends had freed from the palace. Now they were armed and rushing into the wheat farm. They fought the griefers. Violet Ender Pearled away to the tree house and grabbed the enchanted armor, then Ender Pearled back and put the armor on.

"Surrender!" demanded the woman in the red jumpsuit.

"Destroy them!" Daniel ordered his army.

"It's over, Daniel," the woman screamed.

"Never!" cried Daniel.

"We have a bigger army." She smiled at Violet.

The entire town was wearing diamond armor and invading the wheat farm to battle the rainbow griefers. Daniel was outnumbered.

Violet turned Kyle and Will back to survival mode from hardcore.

Then she took the apple the griefer had forced her to steal and transformed it into a golden apple.

She handed it to a townsperson who was being clobbered by Daniel.

As the townspeople attacked, many of the griefers didn't bother fighting back. Instead they just sprinted out of town.

"Where's Daniel?" Noah asked as he searched through the crowd for the ringleader behind the town's invasion.

Nobody could find him. Violet saw purple mist and knew Daniel had escaped.

"It might be," Hannah answered, "but so long as he isn't hurting anyone, he's not our problem anymore."

One of the townspeople approached and invited Violet and her friends to a celebratory dinner.

The group feasted. Another blast was heard in the distance. This one wasn't as loud.

"The sound of destruction is growing farther away," remarked Ben.

Violet devoured a piece of cake. "This is the best day ever."

Ben wanted to agree, but he had searched the town and couldn't find his dog anywhere. He couldn't help but be sad. "I can't find Hope."

"The dog has to be somewhere in the village," said Violet.

Just then Hannah walked over, with Hope trailing behind her, "Look who I found!"

Hope began to bark and Ben was happily reunited with his dog.

The sun was setting, and Violet quickly constructed a crude cabin. When they were all safely in bed, she thought about the enchanted book in her inventory and how helpful it would be for protecting the town. She was glad she had kept it from Daniel. The next morning when she woke up, she would be rebuild. There weren't any rainbow griefers to battle. There was a smile on her face as Violet closed her eyes and dreamt about all the new buildings she'd construct. She had so many ideas, and she was finally free to build and to dream.

THE END

18
REWARDS

The sun began to shine as Violet walked off the wheat farm and looked over the peaceful town. She passed the palace rubble. Everything seemed so quiet without the rainbow griefers terrorizing everybody. Violet stopped at the water and looked up at the spot in the trees where she and Noah used to live.

"I can't believe it's over," Noah said as he approached Violet.

"We want to thank you." Kyle walked over with her husband.

"I want to help you rebuild," added Hannah.

The townspeople all came together to thank Violet.

"It wasn't me who saved this village. It was you. You were the ones who saved us." Violet looked out at the town.

Noah added, "Now that we are free of Daniel and his evil rainbow griefer army, we have to rebuild this village together. Let's promise each other this will be a peaceful place to live."

"What about hostile mobs?" asked Ben.

"We will battle those together," said Violet.

"Should we look for Daniel?" the woman in the red jumpsuit asked. "I don't want him coming back and causing any more trouble."

"I think we should focus on rebuilding the town. I've had enough fighting for now," Violet replied and then asked, "Does everybody agree?"

The town agreed; they were ready to start rebuilding and enjoying their freedom again.

The vibe in the village was festive. There was talk of a victory party. Noah stood next to Violet.

"I know you're upset that your tree house was destroyed, but now you have a chance to build another one." Noah eyed another large tree that stood by the water.

"I'd love to live in a tree house," said the woman in the red jumpsuit.

Violet looked over at her, "I can build one for you. I am a pretty good builder. But you never told me your name."

"It's Angela," the woman replied.

"I'm Violet." She smiled.

"I already knew who you were," said Angela, nodding. "Everyone knows that you are one of the best builders in the Overworld."

Violet blushed. "I'm glad that I can build again. I hope my new buildings will attract a lot of people to this town, so we'll have people to trade our resources with."

"I'm happy life is back to normal," added Noah.

A blast was heard in the distance.

"Do you think that's Daniel?" Ben sprinted over when he heard the explosion.

DO YOU LIKE FICTION FOR MINECRAFTERS?

Check out other unofficial Minecrafter
adventures from Sky Pony Press!

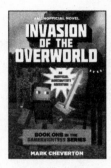

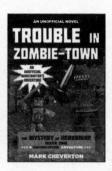

Invasion of the
Overworld
MARK CHEVERTON

Battle for the
Nether
MARK CHEVERTON

Confronting the
Dragon
MARK CHEVERTON

Trouble in
Zombie-town
MARK CHEVERTON

The Quest for
the Diamond
Sword
WINTER MORGAN

The Mystery
of the Griefer's
Mark
WINTER MORGAN

The Endermen
Invasion
WINTER MORGAN

Treasure
Hunters in
Trouble
WINTER MORGAN

Available wherever books are sold!

LIKE OUR BOOKS FOR MINECRAFTERS?

Then check out other novels
by Sky Pony Press.

Pack of Dorks
BETH VRABEL

**Boys Camp:
Zack's Story**
CAMERON DOKEY,
CRAIG ORBACK

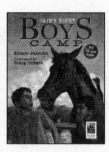

**Boys Camp:
Nate's Story**
KITSON JAZYNKA,
CRAIG ORBACK

**Letters from an
Alien Schoolboy**
R. L. ASQUITH

**Just a Drop of
Water**
KERRY O'MALLEY
CERRA

Future Flash
KITA HELMETAG
MURDOCK

Sky Run
ALEX SHEARER

Mr. Big
CAROL AND MATT
DEMBICKI

Available wherever books are sold!